I0457434

A PREQUEL STORY IN
THE DEMON DIARIES

CLAIRE CHILTON

First published in Great Britain by Ragz Books 2013

This edition published by Ragz Books 2017

Published in Great Britain by Ragz Books

ISBN-10: 1-908822-38-4
ISBN-13: 978-1-908822-38-3

Bibliography

Voltaire, The Works of Voltaire: A Contemporary
Version with Notes, Volume 41, USA, E. R. Du
Mont, 1901.

MORE BOOKS

THE DEMON DIARIES
A Hint of Magic
Bewitched by Magic

Demonic Dora
Bewitched in Hell

Deceased Dora
Bewitched in Death

Divine Dora
Bewitched in Heaven

A Hint of Hell
Bewitched by Christmas

"Illusion is the first of all pleasures."
(L'illusion est le premier plaisir.)

– *The Maid of Orleans*
(La Pucelle d'Orléans),
Voltaire (1901).

CONFESSION

Dora Carridine shifted uncomfortably on the hard wooden seat of confessional, staring blankly at the red velvet curtain in front of her. She glanced sideways at the wooden grate and sighed.

This is going to suck.

"Tell me your sins, child."

She recognized her father's voice and shook her head. "What, all of them?"

"Just this week will do." Her father, the reverend Theodore Carridine, snapped on the other side of the grate.

"I forgot to do the dishes again," she said.

"Did you confess to your mother?"

"No, I was hoping she wouldn't notice."

"Lying is a sin."

"So is making me wash up after curry night." She idly twirled her combat knife in her hands.

"No it isn't!"

"Are you sure?" She grinned as she heard her father lose his cool. It was nice to see a human side to the good reverend. Most of the time, he seemed more like a preacher than a dad to her.

"It's not in the scripture."

"Neither is day dreaming over Taylor Lautner, but you said that was a sin," she mumbled as she slipped the knife back into the scabbard inside her black biker boots.

"What?"

"Nothing." She played with the frayed edge of her black mini-skirt and attempted to sound innocent.

"Have you been having sexual thoughts?" her father asked

She grimaced. "Eww! I'm not telling you that." She noticed the shadow of her father shake his head.

2

"Fine. What other sins do you need to confess?"

"I stole a cookie out of your lunch box last week."

"Which one?"

"The Oreo."

"Damnit Dora, I love those ones. Why would you do that?"

"Mom didn't give me any cookies."

"Do you think you deserve cookies?"

"Everyone deserves cookies."

Her father growled. "What else?"

She sighed. "It was me who broke the TV. I sneaked into a nightclub with Ellie last week and met a boy. Oh, and I joined a demon worshipping forum online."

"WHAT!" She heard a thud in the other booth and suspected her father had just dropped his bible.

"Well, you asked. Now can I be forgiven, so we can get this over with?"

"What forum? I'll have them shut down. What boy?"

"Oh just some random forum, and I dunno what his name was. He was just a guy. He seemed nice when he took me for a ride on his Hog."

"*You* are beyond saving."

"That's not how it works."

"You're grounded for a month. Get out and pray for forgiveness fifty times and then go to your room!"

"Fine, but don't blame me if next week I have to confess to breaking out of my room," she said as she opened the curtain and stepped out into her father's church. She smiled as she walked down the aisle towards the ornate wooden doors, listening to him roar behind her.

I'm not asking for forgiveness. Serves him right for being a dick.

"Dora, get back here right now!" Her father bellowed.

She glanced back and saw him scramble out of the confession box. His face was red with anger, and his vestments were in disarray. She kept walking away and ignored him.

"Satan's spawn," he cried.

She scowled as she opened the doors and stepped out into the bright sunlight. She'd heard that phrase too many times as a child, and it grated on her nerves. She stomped down the stone steps, ripping new ladders in her torn black tights along the way.

She didn't understand why her parents disliked her so much. But they had their own idea of what kind of daughter they wanted, and she wasn't it. She liked gothic and dark things. But most of all, she liked magic. She wanted the world to be a place where mystical things would happen rather than the mundane one she lived in. Unfortunately, she could always see the illusion behind the magic. Her father was a televangelist, and it was all illusion in her eyes.

Maybe there is no such thing as magic.

"DEMON!" Her father screamed behind her as she made her way down the street, heading for the woods while trying to ignore his demands and insults.

She sighed as she left the street and headed onto the woodland trail, leaving the church and her father behind. She needed to get away from all of this and find a place of her own.

Birds chirped around her, and the sun burned down through the trees. She sighed, trying to appreciate the beauty around her, but failing dismally.

I wish I was free.

Dora lay on the grass by the lake, stretching out in the sunlight and staring up at the clear blue skies above her. To an observer, she may have looked peaceful, but inside she was burning with anger. The more she thought about her parents and her life, the angrier she became. Life was not supposed to be like this. People weren't supposed to be trapped in a life they didn't choose. She was expected to be a better daughter, but no one expected her parents to be better parents. She felt powerless and alone, and that made her angrier.

She stood up and scowled at the lake. The world should allow for people to be different. The world should let people be free. She couldn't count the amount of times she'd prayed to God for help over the years, but he had never answered. Perhaps it was time she looked to someone else for assistance.

Feeling the need to do something, she ripped the crucifix from around her neck and gripped it tightly in her fist. Her father had given her this when she was five years old, and for all of *his* sins, she had never taken it off or given up on him. She knew that she couldn't go on any longer pretending that life would get better.

God helps those who help themselves, right?

She wasn't going to wait for help any longer. She was going to demand it.

She glanced down at the delicate gold necklace that glinted in her hand and then she gritted her teeth. Exhaling, she glared at the crucifix.

"I call upon the armies of Heaven and Hell to assist me. I'll do anything to change this awful life. I don't care who I worship. I'll serve the one who serves me," she cried as she threw the cross into the lake with all her might.

She watched it fly across the slick surface before it plunked into the murky waters in the distance. She stared at the ever-decreasing circles that were rippling around where the necklace had landed, waiting for some kind of sign that her message had been heard.

After a moment of silence, the gentle summer breeze blew strands of her ebony hair across her cheek. She lowered her head.

Of course it didn't work. Nothing ever works.

She frowned as shadows appeared on the grass around her. Darkness engulfed the lake. She looked up at the sky in awe as a looming black cloud appeared above her.

Did it work?

She felt her hopes rise when the cloud rumbled. Something was about to change. She could feel it. The air was dense with a dark presence.

Yes, show me the way.

A blob of cold rain splatted on her forehead, and she frowned. Then another one did. She narrowed her eyes and stared across the lake as a downpour came from the cloud and drenched her in an instant with cold, soggy rain. She felt a dribble of cold water run down her nose and splash off it onto her chest.

Well, fuck you too.

She sank to her knees and scowled at the lake.

Nothing is ever going to change.

Exhaling a disappointed sigh, she blankly peered down at the chipped, black polish on her nails.

She frowned when they became misty as a subtle fog drifted over her. Containing a shiver as an icy breeze brushed across her wet skin, she felt her hopes begin to rise again.

Don't even go there, idiot. It's always colder when you're wet, and fog is just fog.

Ignoring her natural inclination to see magic where there was just illusion, she stood up and turned away from the lake, deciding to make her way home. Her heart was heavy as she acknowledged her disappointment in the universe. Her boots squelched on the wet grass, making her feel even more depressed. She didn't glance back at the lake as she left the park.

Life sucks!

The mist surrounded the lake before it turned green. It swirled behind her in a trail as it followed her out of the park.

A QUEST FOR MAGIC

The next morning, Dora followed her mother through the busy streets at a snail's pace. She watched her mother's coiffed blonde hair swing around her head as she purposefully strode down the main street a few yards ahead of her.

"Hurry up, Dora. We can't be late for your father's show." Her mother turned her head and called over her shoulder.

Dora dragged her feet, scuffing her Doc Martins on the sidewalk and scowling at her mother's back.

I don't want to go. I'm tired of church services and happy-clapping bullshit.

Being the daughter of a preacher wasn't easy, but

being the daughter of a televangelist was so much worse. She wasn't even sure if she believed in God. For an almighty being, he hadn't made her world very magical.

She glanced down at the shopping bags in her hands. The arm of a pink fluffy cardigan hung out of one of them. Narrowing her eyes, she scuffed it against the bricks of the building beside her, dragging it so the angora wool caught and pulled.

"What are you doing?" her mother cried.

Dora glanced up and sighed. *Busted.*

"I just bought you that. Why are you ruining it?" Her mother rushed over to her and snatched the bags out of her hands. "You're going to confession for this!" She snapped before spinning on her heel and storming ahead.

What, again? Not bloody likely. And, I hate pink fluffy cardigans. Dog vomit would look nicer on me.

Dora shook her head. She knew she was being obnoxious, but she hated her life. She hated church, she hated pink fluffy things, and she really hated confession. She enjoyed magic and mystery. She wanted to live in a world where she could be herself without having to explain it. The darkness was exciting. It was free. She just wanted to live how she chose.

She blankly stared ahead at her mother, who was rushing past the entrance to a dark alley. While focusing on the dingy alley that was squashed between the mini-market and the opticians, she frowned.

Most people wouldn't even notice it existed. It was so narrow and dark that it could be mistaken for a shadow. But she knew it was a shortcut to the rundown side of town, which only the locals knew about.

"Hurry up. Don't let your father down, again," her mother called out behind her.

Dora scowled again. It never seemed to matter what she wanted. All that ever mattered was what her parents wanted.

She eyed the entrance of the alley as a greenish mist exuded from it, and she watched the smoke billow downwards into the gutter. Making a decision that today things were going to change, she turned towards the passage. She'd always tried to please her parents. Okay, she failed dismally at it, but she'd always tried. Not once had they ever tried to please her.

Peering at her mother to ensure she wasn't watching, she slipped into the alley and ran down it as fast as she could.

Her Docs thumped against the cobbled stones as she raced into the darkness towards the side of town that everyone had told her to avoid.

She realized that the green steam must be coming from one of the many vents as it floated around her feet, wafting around her and making the air denser.

Ignoring it, she rushed through the fog. She wanted to see the darker side of life. She wanted to find a new world where she would finally belong.

The walls were slimy with moss and grime. She carefully avoided touching them as she slowed near the dingy light at the end of the passage.

Hitching her breath, she peered out into the ramshackle street. Unlike the busier shopping streets, this one was dark and empty. No lights shone in the windows of the oddly-named stores.

Her heart pounded as she stepped out of the alley

and into the street. She waited for a moment for something to happen, but nothing did. With a sigh of relief, she walked down the street at a relaxed pace, taking in the sights around her with wide eyes.

Gold 'n' Brass was the first store she passed. Contained behind the grimy window were antiques and a jumble of random items. She paused at a section of wedding rings that were displayed in a cracked glass case, frowning at them with a feeling of disappointment. Marriage, it seemed, was not eternal as her father often told her it was. Judging by the price tags, you could purchase other people's for nine ninety-nine. She gazed at the array of personal items on sale, feeling sad. It was like browsing through people's lost lives.

She shook her head and carried on walking down the street. She didn't know what she was looking for, but it felt as if she was searching for something that would give her life meaning. Deep inside, she knew that this was the place she would find her answers.

Her stomach turned as she passed a dingy café. The doors were shut, but there was a stand outside of it offering a 'heart attack sandwich', which appeared to be filled with greasy pork. She continued past it to the next shop, feeling a bit queasy.

The next building was older than the others were and appeared to be subsiding at an angle. The doorway was tiny, and the window ledge was too close to the ground. Behind the glass were unusual-looking books, bound in hide rather than card. Strange symbols hung down the window. Dream catchers and candle flames were blowing around inside as if propelled through the air by some kind of phantom breeze.

She took a step closer to the store window and peered inside. Jars filled with powders and twisted roots lined the shelves inside. The store appeared to be lit by hundreds of different colored candles. She glanced up at the sign above the door that creaked as it idly swung in the breeze. The store was called 'Dark Gifts', and it appeared to be a magic store.

This is it! This is what I've been looking for, she realized as she peered at the array of magical items in the store window.

With a shiver of fear, she opened the door. A small bell jingled above it announcing her presence. Green-tinged smoke billowed through the doorway and into the street. She watched the mist in awe before gritting her teeth and taking a tentative step inside.

"Hello?" She called out as she walked into the shop. Her footsteps echoed on the stone floor as she walked through the aisles of mystical statues, tarots and herbs. The room was large and dimly lit with several aisles of odd-looking items mingling on shelves beside strange books. There were jars with slimy creatures in them and strange plants she had never seen before. She headed towards the golden talismans on the back wall. Not really knowing what she was looking for.

"Hello." Dora jumped as a female voice whispered in her ear.

She spun around to see a large woman with flaming red hair standing behind her. She scanned the woman, her eyes widening at the sight of her emerald robe, which was embroidered with silver and gold thread. Her hair was a bush of red frizzy fire, and her eyes were catlike green.

"How can I help you?" Her voice was soft and melodic, which calmed Dora's frazzled nerves.

"I, er … I'm not sure what I'm looking for." Dora managed as the woman stared intently at her.

"Perhaps I can help if you tell me what troubles you." The woman brushed back a wisp of hair from her face with a bejeweled hand. Silver, gold and emerald rings decorated every finger.

Dora stared at the bracelet on the shopkeeper's wrist that was overflowing with charms. She tried to put her feelings into words.

Everything messes with me. There's not one thing in the world that doesn't fuck with me on a daily basis.

She shook her head, trying to think of something to say. "I want power," she blurted.

The woman lowered her eyes to her hand. She slowly turned the ring on her wedding finger, remaining silent. Eventually, she looked up at Dora again. "Power comes with a price."

Dora considered the five bucks she had in her purse and stared back at the shopkeeper. "How much?"

A glint of light sparked in the shopkeeper's already bright eyes. "Perhaps more than you can pay."

17

Dora decided to throw caution to the wind. What did she have to lose, right?

"Is there an ATM around here?" She had been saving up her allowance for weeks. There was at least fifty bucks in there.

"I don't need your money." The shopkeeper waved away her question.

"Then er, what do you want?" Dora began to feel a tad uncomfortable.

The shopkeeper tilted her head and flashed a wicked smile. "How far are you willing to go for power? Would you dance with the devil?"

She considered the question for a moment. She hadn't even danced with a guy before. All the boys at her school refused to dance. She never had a boyfriend, so she couldn't force one to dance with her like the other girls did. "What like, slow dancing?" she asked.

"Any kind of dancing. The kind doesn't matter," the shopkeeper said.

"Well, I dunno. I mean if the Devil asked me to River Dance, it might be a bit of a problem. I don't think my legs move that fast." She tried not to imagine the Devil River Dancing across a stage, but it was too late. The image was already firmly lodged in her mind.

"Not bloody River Dancing." The shopkeeper shook her head.

"Well then, yeah okay. I won't mind dancing with the devil," Dora said.

IN THE DARK

"**M**y name is Loanda." The shopkeeper offered her hand, and Dora reluctantly shook it. "If you wish to have more power, then I can help you."

She eyed Loanda, releasing her hand and wondering what exactly she was offering her.

"How, are you a witch?"

Loanda scowled. "We prefer the term Goddesses of the Light."

"What light if you dance with the Devil?"

"The Devil is grossly misunderstood." Loanda twirled the pendant around her neck. "We worship the good in all, even the Devil."

"How's that working out for you?" Dora asked,

skeptical at the idea of a good devil.

"We've conjured many things from the shadows in our world. If you truly want to experience real magic, then we can show you that."

"We?" She glanced around, wondering if Loanda was just a crazy person who had several imaginary friends.

"My coven is the most powerful in all of Berkville. Together we will imbue magic and light upon this dismal world." Loanda's eyes seemed to glow as she beamed at her.

"Aren't you the only coven in Berkville?"

Loanda coughed, ignoring the question. "The coven—"

"Are they here now?" Dora butted in. She looked around again, assuming they were figments of the woman's imagination when she didn't see anyone else in the store.

"No. We meet at the witching hour."

Dora breathed a sigh.

Wait, a real coven of witches, here in Berkville!

She shivered again, but this time with excitement. If what Loanda said was true, then there was real magic in the world that she could experience. "Okay, how do I join your coven?"

Loanda laughed and shook her head in a condescending manner. "Silly child, you cannot simply join us as if it were a youth club. You must prove your worth before we will even consider you."

"By dancing with the devil?" Dora asked.

"By completing three trials.

She studied the witch, and a part of her brain was screaming for her to leave the store and never come back. There was something odd about the woman and her offer. But she lived in a religious bubble, and she was frowned upon by everyone. Witchcraft was something she wanted to believe in. She didn't believe in much, but magic just had to exist. If she could be a witch, then she wouldn't be the black sheep of the town anymore. Well, at least she could curse anyone who called her one. At the end of the day, it felt right to be here. Something had guided her here. All she had to do was follow her instincts, right?

"What do you want me to do?"

Loanda turned and gave a dramatic wave, pointing

towards a small door at the back of the room.

Dora turned to examine the door. It appeared to be made of ancient oak, and there were strange symbols carved into the wood.

"Follow me."

She followed Loanda, feeling apprehensive as the witch reached the door and placed a small golden key into the lock before turning it. Loanda pushed open the door and led her into a dark room.

She squinted when Loanda flipped the switch and turned on the electric lights. Her eyes widened as she stared at the vast pentagram that was painted on the floor in what looked like blood. Black candles resided at every point of the star. A podium stood behind the pentagram, and resting upon it was an ancient book that was decorated with sigils and symbols.

Unfortunately, that was where the magic of the room ended. Surrounding the mystical centerpiece was a stockroom filled with boxes of mass-produced magical goods.

Dora read one of the banners emblazoned on the side of the box nearest to her.

CLAIRE CHILTON
CURSE YOUR BOYFRIEND WITH A VOODOO DOLL!
CURSE–O–MATIC™ PRODUCTS ARE FOR ENTERTAINMENT PURPOSES ONLY AND ARE SAFETY APPROVED.

She shook her head.

Are you shitting me?

She glanced up to find Loanda studying her through slitted eyes.

She offered a brief smile that the witch didn't return. "Okay, so how does this thing work?"

"We must complete a dark initiation to imbue you with power. There are dangers, but I will guide you through them. If you are worthy of the dark gift, then your trials will begin. If you pass each trial, then you will become a Goddess of the Light, and the coven will welcome you." Loanda walked towards the podium and opened the grimoire that resided upon it.

Dora jumped when the heavy book thumped against the wooden stand, and the noise to echoed through the room. "We...we're going to do it now?"

"Yes," Loanda said as she lit the black candle

beside her.

"What do I need to do?"

"Stand in the center of the pentagram and face north."

Dora inhaled deeply before stepping onto the pentagram. She positioned herself in the center and then paused. She turned to face Loanda. "Er, which way is north?"

Loanda rolled her eyes for a moment and muttered something under her breath.

"What?" Dora asked.

"Just face the boxes of Twinkies," Loanda snapped.

She turned to face the stacks of indestructible pastries, wondering why they were in the stockroom of a magic shop. "Do you sell a lot of magical Twinkies, then?"

"They make great snacks after summoning a demon. Lots of carbs."

"You know that carbs don't do anything good for you, right?"

"Our bodies are temples that are protected by our power," Loanda said, wearing a serene smile.

She eyed Loanda's bulging belly, but decided to remain silent.

"Are you ready?" Loanda's soothing voice returned.

"As ever," Dora said, wondering if this was going to be as craptastic as it felt.

"Feel the power inside you. Feel the power around you and draw it into yourself. Look into the world and see the veil that covers your eyes. Lift that veil."

Dora stared at the boxes of Twinkies. The brown cardboard was dull to watch. She tried to feel power inside of herself but could only feel her breathing. She tried to feel the power around her. Her surroundings were cramped and too warm. Beads of sweat popped up on her brow. She shot a sideways glance at Loanda.

The witch was reading silently from the book. Her lips were moving, but no sound came out.

She stared back at the Twinkies, trying to see a veil over them. She tried to imagine inside the box, but her mind only came up with an image of more Twinkies.

"How do you feel?" Loanda asked.

"It's a bit hot in here." She swiped her forehead with her hand to wipe away the moisture that had gathered there.

"You have looked into the fires of Hell, child," Loanda said. "It's working."

Dora frowned.

Did I? Because it felt as if I just looked into a box of Twinkies.

"Ommmneeeeee!" Loanda cried.

Dora jumped when the room went dark. She spun around, but could only see inky darkness around her. "What the hell?"

When lights came back on a few moments later, she saw Loanda holding an ancient-looking piece of parchment in her chubby hand. The paper was folded and sealed with wax. "You have passed. You are now imbued with the dark gift," she said, waving the letter at her.

"What's that?"

"This is your first trial, something you must read carefully. I cannot help you after this point, but I have imbued you with enough power to complete your task. Take care, young one, for this is instruction from the Devil himself. Do not fail him." She handed her the letter.

Dora stared at the yellowing parchment. It was burnt around the edges and warm to touch. A shiver shot down her spine.

Did this really come from Hell?

TRIALS AND TEMPTATION

Dora stared down at the hex bag in her hand. It was a tiny, cloth sack tied with twine and leaves of some kind. It definitely had something in it judging by the weight of it. The object inside felt hard and rectangle-shaped.

Loanda had given it to her with a warning. She was not allowed to open it, or she would be cursed by it too. Although she was dying to look inside, she managed to refrain and shoved the bag into the back pocket of her jeans with a shake of her head. She had a mission to complete.

She tugged the baseball cap down, so it shadowed her eyes. Then she gritted her teeth as she walked towards the entrance of the huge skyscraper, which from the outside appeared to be mostly made of glass. As she walked through the open doors into a large reception area, she gripped the green paper bag of food that she held in her hands. She glanced down. The logo for 'Thai Garden' emblazoned on the bag of food matched the logo on her cap and T-shirt.

She approached the reception desk and held her breath. Her nerves were rattled just by being here.

I hope no one notices that this shirt is too big for me.

She'd borrowed the uniform from Hal. He was probably the most laid-back guy at school. Luckily he'd been laid-back enough not to ask why she wanted his shirt.

The woman behind the reception desk was an icy blonde, wearing a sharp gray suit that matched her sharp gray eyes.

Dora shot a sideways glance towards the board next to the reception desk. It listed the companies inside the building. Cabot Investments was marked as being on the third floor.

"Ahem." The blonde coughed, and Dora turned to face her. "Can I help you?"

"Delivery for Howard Delaney at Cabot Investments," Dora replied, trying to act like a delivery person.

The receptionist narrowed her eyes. "It's a bit early for lunch."

Shit, shit, shit... She inwardly panicked, but outwardly shrugged. "What can I tell you, the guy wants his sushi now," she said, keeping her voice as relaxed as possible.

"Fine, take it up. Third floor. Check in with reception there." The blonde pointed towards the lifts behind her.

Dora nodded and headed towards the lifts. She pressed the call button and stared at the chrome doors. Getting past the second receptionist was going to be a nightmare. She needed to get into Howard's office if she was going to plant the hex bag there.

The lift doors finally opened, and she stepped into the elevator before pressing three on the dashboard. She pulled her cell phone out of her pocket once the doors closed, and the lift began moving. She needed help with this one. She dialed Loanda's number and pressed call.

"May the light be with you," Loanda said when she answered.

"Hey, it's Dora. I need your help."

"How may I guide you?" Loanda's soothing tone echoed through the phone.

"Guide me past the receptionist on the third floor. How do I get into Howard's office?"

"Lie your way in," Loanda said in a less soothing tone.

"What the fuck am I supposed to say? I'm delivering sushi, not gold bullion."

"Get creative. This is your trial, and I'm not here to do it for you."

"Gee thanks," she muttered as Loanda hung up on her. She scowled at the phone before dropping it back into her jeans pocket. "I guess I'm on my own," she said to herself.

Her heart hammered as the doors opened to reveal another reception desk. Luckily, this one was empty. She made a dash down the corridor to her left, hoping it was the right direction. She moved fast until she was out of sight of the reception area, exhaling a breath of relief when she found herself in an empty corridor. She passed many doors with plaques on them as she wandered down the corridor, pausing briefly to scan the names on them.

The corridor widened. She lowered her head as she passed a glass meeting room with people inside it. She shot a sideways glance at them, but no one took notice of her. Inside the room, a tall man with gray hair was shouting at a group of people. Most of them were nodding, except a younger man at the back who was scowling at him while viciously sharpening a pencil.

Dora hurried past to the next corridor of offices, pausing only to read the nameplates on the doors. She came to a stop outside the door marked 'Howard Delaney – Finance Assistant'. She wondered idly what he'd done to incur the wrath of Hell, but shrugged. Loanda had told her that he deserved his fate.

She pressed her ear to the door. There was a strange squealing sound coming from inside the room. Images of a wild boar being slaughtered jumped into her mind. She shuddered at the thought and stepped away from the door, looking around for somewhere to hide. There was an alcove to her right, which was shadowed enough to conceal her. When a shriek came from the office, she jumped back and rushed into the alcove, pressing her back against the wall.

Howard's door swung open. Dora gulped, expecting a bloody mess to walk out of the office. Instead a disheveled blonde in tight pink dress stepped out of the room, tugging her skirt down and adjusting her bra. Dora frowned as a man in his late thirties followed the woman through the doorway. His shirt was unbuttoned halfway, and his tie hung loosely around his collar.

That was their sex noises!

Dora widened her eyes. She hadn't ever had sex herself, but she was pretty sure she wasn't going to sound like a squealing pig when she eventually did.

"Let's go to lunch, sugar." The man tightened his tie and straightened his shirt.

"Okay, Howie. Can we go to the Italian place?" The woman's voice was squeaky to a point of annoying.

"Sure thing, babe." He wrapped an arm around

her waist and led her down the corridor, straight past where Dora was hiding.

Dora watched the couple leave.

That's what he does at work? No wonder he's in trouble.

She stepped out of the alcove and into the corridor, staring at the open office door while deep in thought. She'd never been in an office before, but it seemed the whole purpose of being in one was to look sharp, shout at people and fuck around.

I wonder if they teach that at university?

"Hey, are you lost?" A male voice made her jump as it interrupted her thoughts.

She spun around to face a boy who appeared to be her age. He had bright blue eyes and dark hair. He wore a white T-shirt and jeans. Her brain froze in fear of being caught as he stood behind a cart that was full of mail, waiting silently for her to reply. She shook herself out of her daze. "Um, what?"

A smile broke across his face, lighting it up. "I asked if you were lost."

"I er, no. No, I know where I'm going." She managed. The guy was hot. It was distracting.

"Okay, well, let me know if I can help. This place is full of evil," he said.

"What?" She widened her eyes.

What the hell have I walked into?

"You know, the suits." He pointed to a man walking by in a tailored suit, who was carrying a black leather briefcase. The man didn't acknowledge their presence as he continued past them. "We have to stick together," the mail guy said with a wink.

"Oh, yeah." She nodded, trying to think of a way to get rid of him.

"Work placement?" he asked.

Her brain seemed to have shut down, but she tried to force it to work. "What, at school?"

"Yeah, you're a sophomore, right?"

Dora nodded, even though she was a year and many exams away from being a sophomore, assuming she even got that far. Her current grades indicated that she'd never get past freshman year, and she could expect to have a wonderful job in the custodial arts, possibly cleaning nightclub toilets. "Yep, work placement." She lied.

"Cool, me too," he said. "Oh, and crap. I'm

Jamie, by the way. Nice to meet you." He held out his hand.

She shook his hand, feeling a warm tingle inside when she touched him. "I'm, um." She paused, trying to decide if it was wise to give her real name.

"Um?" He raised an eyebrow.

"Uma." She lied.

"It's nice to meet you, Uma. When you're done here, do you want to grab a bite to eat?" Jamie asked.

"Yeah, sure." She almost kicked herself.

What am I doing? This is so stupid!

He smiled again.

He is kind of cute though.

"What about Joe's Deli over the road? Meet in about an hour?" he asked.

"Sounds good." She nodded, wondering what mess she was about to get herself into by talking to him.

"See you later." He winked before turning to push his cart down the corridor.

Oh, great move dumbass. Now you have a witness.

She shook her head at her own idiocy before

turning back to face Howard's office. She pushed open the door and peered inside. As expected, the office was empty.

Dora stepped into the room and quickly crossed it in a couple of strides, glancing briefly at the couch that was in disarray with cushions hanging off it. She frowned before rushing behind Howard's desk and opening the top drawer. She quickly dropped the hex bag into the drawer and pushed it to the back, so it wouldn't be seen.

Mission accomplished.

Her cell phone vibrated in her back pocket. She pulled it out and peered at the caller. *Loanda.* "Hello." She answered the call.

"Is it done?" Loanda sounded excited.

Dora walked out of the office, dropping the sushi bag in a trashcan on her way out. "Yes."

"Congratulations on your first trial. You need to come to the store for your next mission." Loanda sounded pleased.

"Okay, but gimme a few hours. I have a couple of things I need to do first."

"Tonight at the witching hour."

"When's that?"

"You don't know when the witching hour is?"

"Er, no."

"Midnight!"

"Oh, okay. I have a curfew though."

"Are you shitting me?"

"Forget it. I'll be there." She wasn't too worried. How hard could sneaking out of her room be, after all? Anyway, she wanted Loanda off the phone. She was looking forwards to meeting Jamie.

DATING DISASTERS

Dora strolled into Joe's Deli and paused at the doorway, scanning the crowded tables for Jamie. She frowned when she didn't see him and considered leaving.

It was a stupid idea anyway. I should just go home.

She turned to leave, but bumped face-first into a muscled chest. "Oh shit, sorry," she mumbled into it.

"Don't be. It's a nice surprise. You know you can come out of there now if you want to." Jamie's familiar voice said into the top of her head, his hot breath warming her hair.

Dora jumped back and peered up at him. "You seem taller," she said after she'd gathered her wits.

"Really? Because you seem shorter." He grinned.

She straightened her shoulders, so she was her full height. "I'd tower over you in heels."

"I dunno, I kinda like the Docs." He winked as he took her arm. "So, shall we get a table, or were you leaving?"

"I suppose we could get a table." She flashed him a smile.

"Let's grab one at the back. I hate sitting in the window," he said as he led her through the busy tables to the booths at the back of the café.

My thoughts exactly.

"Sounds good," she mumbled as she slid into a booth at the back of the room. It was cozy with brown padded seats and dim lighting over the oak table.

"It sucks doing all these tasks, doesn't it?" Jamie said.

"What?" She panicked.

Does he know about the trials?

"Work experience. I thought it would be fun, but being the mail boy sucks. You know how many whining suits I have to deal with?"

41

"Ohh yeah, the tasks suck." She nodded.

"Is yours all deliveries?" he asked.

"Yep." She nodded again, unsure of what to say.

"Really? You don't have to make the food or serve it, or anything?" He raised his eyebrows in surprise. "When my friend Billy worked for Pizza Hut, he did everything at some point or another.

"Guess I'm lucky." She lied, realizing that this date was going to be more difficult than she'd imagined.

"Well, you certainly brightened my day by visiting the office today, so I think I'm the lucky one."

Her heart felt as if it had expanded in her chest. Boys never spoke to her like this. Mostly they just played pranks on her or called her names. She'd never met a nice one before, and it was causing all kinds of strange reactions inside her. She'd always assumed she was too odd to date.

Is he flirting with me? D'ho, he did ask you on a date.

She found it difficult to rationalize someone liking her, so she felt suspicious of everything he said. "Um, glad I could help," she mumbled.

He chuckled and offered her the menu. "Let's get some food. I'm starving."

She nodded. "Okay. I could eat something." She peered at the menu. A feeling of being watched nagged at her, and goosebumps appeared on her arms. She glanced over the top of the menu, surprised to meet Jamie's bright blue eyes. He was intently watching her with a look that sent shivers up and down her spine. "Er, what?" she asked.

"What?"

"What are you staring at?"

"You," he said, continuing to stare.

"Er, why?"

"Because you're beautiful."

She blinked and tried to think straight, but it was impossible when he was looking at her like that and saying things like that to her. "What? Don't be silly."

His expression broke into a smile. "And so innocent about it. Why is it silly to call you beautiful?"

"I dunno. I'm used to being called Satan's Spawn." She shrugged.

"What the hell?" He gasped.

She cringed for a moment, realizing that normal people didn't say that. He was probably a normal boy, and she knew she was far from normal. "Just kidding!" She blurted, trying to cover up her mistake.

"Oh, I see." He relaxed and picked up the second menu on the table.

She glanced back at her menu and hid behind it.

Good going, idiot. I bet he can't wait to see you again.

"I think I'll get a milkshake and some fries," she said, trying to break the uncomfortable silence that had settled over them.

"Do you want to go out again." He blurted at the same time.

She gulped. "What?"

"The movies or something?" He appeared nervous for the first time.

"Er, do *you* want to?" She was unsure given the odd vibes and uncomfortable silences between them.

"Yeah, of course. Why do you think I asked?"

"Okay." A feeling of hope appeared in her for the first time. Jamie seemed nice, and he seemed to like her. At the very least, she might make a new friend, but it could turn out to be more.

"Tomorrow night?" he asked, looking hopeful.

"Okay, yes. The Movie-Plex?" She was already planning what to wear for her first proper date.

What do normal people do on those?

"Where else?" He winked while brushing his short dark hair out of his eyes. "I'll pick you up at eight?"

Visions of Jamie meeting her over-zealous father flashed across her mind. They weren't particularly pleasant images. "I'll meet you there."

"Even better." He smiled and waved over a waiter. "Now, let's eat."

She nodded, feeling nervous.

How much am I going to mess this up?

She sighed. She had to survive the witching hour first.

THE COVEN

"**W**here the hell do you think you're going?" Dora froze when her father's voice bellowed behind her. She wasn't in the best position to answer him as she hung out of her bedroom window, reaching for the drainpipe. *Crap!*

She slowly glanced back over her shoulder to see a stern expression on his face. His thick white hair was sticking out all over the place. He appeared to have just got out of bed because he was wearing a burgundy bathrobe, crumpled blue pajamas and burgundy slippers. "What?" she asked, composing an innocent expression.

"Where are you going at this time of night?" He

ground out, locking his jaw in anger.

"What makes you think I'm going anywhere?" she asked as she pushed herself back through her window.

"You're climbing out of your window!"

"There's a bird caught in the rafters. It was making a lot of noise and woke me up. I was trying to free it." She lied.

Her father frowned for a moment before narrowing his eyes. "Then why are you dressed and wearing a coat?"

Crap! She quickly tried to think of an excuse. "It was cold. What kind of girl would I be if I hung out of my window in my nightwear?"

"What kind of girl are you for wearing things like that?" Her father gestured at her red mini-shirt and black tights. "And your face. Didn't your mother tell you to stop wearing all that black make-up around your eyes? You look like a …" He appeared lost for words for a moment. "A circus freak!"

She scowled, and anger burned in the back of her throat. She'd been called a lot of things by her father, but of all the small-minded, uncultured and pathetic comments, this one was the most insulting. She scrambled back through her window and jumped onto her carpet with a thud, turning to face him with fire in her eyes. "What the fuck did you just call me?"

His face paled as she stared him down before a spark of anger lit his eyes. "How dare you speak to your father in tha—"

"Father? That's a joke, right? You're not a father. You're a fail preacher with a pole dancer for a wife and shitty TV show as a job. Oh, and let's not forget your *demon child.*"

"Demon!" he cried, waving his cross at her. "Demon get out!"

"Yeah, yeah. It's getting old now. I wish I was a demon because then I could burn your ass straight into Hell." She screamed. "I hate you!"

"Out damned Satan spawn." Her father waved the cross at her as if warding her off.

"My thoughts exactly," she said as she strolled past him and down the stairs towards the front doors."

She heard him race after her. "Where do you think you're going? Get back here."

She opened the front door of the church and

turned to face him. "Go to Hell!" She shouted before she stormed out of the church and into the dark streets.

Dora sighed as she walked the dark streets of Berkville, heading towards the magic store. She knew there was going to be hell to pay when she went home. A part of her hoped she'd never have to go home again.

Why couldn't I just keep my cool until I was part of the coven? Just two more trials, and I'll be free of my awful parents and awful life.

But after years of religious abuse, she'd reached her limit.

There's gotta be a better place than this to live in.

Unlike most people, she didn't fear the darkness. There was no danger in it because there were no people in it. Empty streets didn't scare her. Other people were the only danger in this world.

She checked her watch. It was quarter to twelve, nearly the witching hour. She rushed down the alley to the magic store as if it was her last vestige of hope, feeling more determined to join the coven than ever. She raced towards it under the soft glow of a full moon.

The store lit up the dark street, its window beaming a fiery light into the darkness. She ran towards it and came to a halt in the bright glow of a hundred lit candles. She tried to open the door to enter the shop, but it was locked.

She frowned and tried the door again. It was definitely locked. After a moment of confusion, she knocked on the old wood and waited.

There was a grinding sound as a small hole opened in the top of the door, and a pair of sharp blue eyes stared out at her. "Who goes there?" A woman's voice asked.

"Er, Dora," she said.

"What's the password?"

"I don't fucking know," Dora said, feeling frustrated. "I'm supposed to meet Loanda here."

"No password. No entry." The opening slammed shut.

"What? Open the bloody door! Where's Loanda? I want to speak to her."

There was a sound of voices inside the shop. She pressed her ear to the door to try to hear what was being said, but it was muffled by the thick oak. She pressed harder to try to make out the individual words as the door opened, which caused her to fall into the shop with a yelp. She landed on the hard tiles with a groan. She peered up at the six women standing over her. They all wore robes, which shrouded their faces.

She realized that one of the women was Loanda as she pushed her hood off her head. This time, Loanda was wearing a ruby robe and matching accessories. The woman beside her removed the hood of her dull black robe to reveal a blonde woman with sharp blue eyes. The other four women also removed their hoods, and their eyes were all fixated on Dora.

"Is she the sacrifice?" A brunette witch with doe eyes asked.

"Don't be stupid, Janet. We only sacrifice virgins! She looks as if she's slept with half the football team." The blonde wearing the black robe said.

"Hey!" Dora spoke up. "What the fuck is that supposed to mean?"

"Yeah, what does that mean, Veronica?" Janet asked the blonde.

"Nice girls don't dress like *that*," Veronica said with a look of distaste as she scanned Dora from head to toe.

Dora scowled as she scrambled to her feet and faced the blonde. The fact that she was a virgin wasn't something she intended to admit to, but like hell she was going to be labeled by this harpie. "Honey, I wouldn't screw the football team if you paid me. I do have some taste, and inbred jocks on steroids don't do it for me."

"Isn't your son a quarterback?" Janet asked Veronica.

Veronica's face flushed red, and she narrowed her eyes at Dora. "How dare yo—"

"ENOUGH!" A voice boomed behind her. Dora spun around and came face-to-face with an angry Loanda. "Dora is here for her trial, which we must conjure from the ether for her. As Goddesses of the Light, our duty is to help the lost find their way. There will be no petty fighting in the coven. Do you understand?"

"Who made you head goddess?" Veronica scowled at Loanda.

"Er, you did," doe-eye Janet said to Veronica.

"Janet, will you stop being so fucking literal!" Veronica turned and snapped at her.

"Well, you did," Janet quietly mumbled, lowering her head.

Loanda placed an arm around Dora, leading her away from the bickering witches. "Sister Veronica of the Light is suffering right now. Her inner pain comes out as anger, but do not let it shadow your view of her. She will be herself again soon," she whispered in her ear as she led her into the back room.

Dora glanced back to see the coven following with Janet and Veronica still bickering behind them.

Hundreds of candles lit the stock room. Some were in candelabras, and others were on shelves scattered around the room. The boxes of stock had been covered by black linen. In the center of the room, the pentagram was lit up by the fiery candlelight. She coughed as incense burned, filling the room with perfumed smoke.

"Goddesses of the Light, take your place in the

circle." Loanda commanded, and the witches each stood on a point of the star. "Dora, please stand in the center of the circle." She motioned for her to stand in the center of the pentagram.

Dora walked between Janet and Veronica to stand at the center of the circle and face North. She vaguely remembered where the Twinkie boxes had been even though the room seemed so different since her last visit.

"Join together," Loanda said.

Each witch held their arms out straight, at an angle and held the hands of the people standing on either side of them. Dora suspected that if she looked down on them, she would see them form the shape of a star.

"Lord of the dark, come into the light and show us the way." Loanda chanted, and the witches all chanted with her. "Join with the Earth, and be free once more. Show the magic of life, and let the sin fall away ..."

Dora frowned. It sounded like one of her father's sermons, which she didn't like very much.

"Take our tribute as your own, and guide her to her destiny."

What? I'm a tribute?

She shivered and glanced at the chanting witches around her. Dark cowls shadowed their eyes, and their chants were monotone. The smoky room seemed to shimmer as a wave of dizziness passed over her. The smoke appeared to have a green tint to it before the candles all blew out and plunged the room into darkness. She shivered as a cold breeze brushed over her bare arms, and she heard a deep laugh of a male voice.

She spun around in the darkness, trying to pinpoint the direction of the laugh, but it only echoed once before it was gone. A light sparked, and she saw Loanda holding a zippo and lighting a candle with it. More candles were lit all around her as the witches all did the same. "Did it work?" she asked.

"Look to the Earth for your answer," Loanda said.

She glanced down and noticed a wax sealed letter at her feet. She bent over and picked up the burnt parchment, glancing at the name on the front of it. 'Dora' was all it said.

"Ooh, open it!" Janet was bouncing with excitement until Veronica slapped her across the back of her head. "Oww! Whatcha do that for?"

Veronica shook her head and sighed.

Dora pressed her thumbnail under the seal to crack it open before unfolding the letter. Her fingers trembled. Her whole body was trembling, shaken by the dark laugh she'd heard.

Was that the devil?

She glanced at the words on the page. They appeared to be written in blood and told her to use the powder of Hell on a sinners robes. Underneath the command, a name and address was scrawled on the parchment. She peered at Loanda, who was holding a tiny cloth bag out towards her. Dora took the bag, narrowing her eyes at Loanda.

Why did she have the powder? Surely it would come to me with the note?

"Complete your trial and return to us tomorrow at the witching hour," Loanda said.

"Um, okay, but I'm having some problems with my parents. Getting out at midnight might be difficult," Dora said.

"Then do it in the morning and come at twelve noon. We will be here for your final trial then."

"But it's Sonia's school play tomorrow," Janet said. "I can't miss it."

Loanda rolled her eyes. "Fine, at six. Is that okay for everyone?"

"I was going to play bridge with the Robinsons, but I suppose I could—" Veronica began.

"Cancel it!" Loanda snapped.

"Whatever, six is fine." Veronica growled and turned away from the group, muttering to herself.

Dora stared at the cloth bag in her hand, wondering if this was all getting a bit too dark, even for her.

Dora eyed the apartment building. It was an old Victorian style building with no security on the door, which was going to make it easier for her to get into. She glanced at the name and address on the parchment: Cassie Sheldon, Apartment 4b.

It was beginning to occur to her that she didn't really know what she was doing to these people. She sighed and glanced back towards an empty bench.

Maybe I just need to think about this for a

moment.

She turned away from the apartment building and took a seat on the bench, enjoying the feel of sunlight on her bare arms and face. Her black camisole and black combats seemed to soak up the heat too, making her warm all over.

Home wasn't getting any worse, but mainly because she'd stayed out of her parents way. They'd been in bed when she snuck in last night, and still there when she snuck out this morning.

Yeah, but how long can I do that for?

But then on the other hand, the witches weren't exactly perfect. The idea of dealing with Veronica for a lifetime wasn't particularly appealing.

It could all be bullshit. Anyone can flip a light switch.

She frowned at the small sack of powder. She didn't even know what it would do, but maybe that was the test. She unsurely tapped the bag against her knee. What she was doing didn't feel right.

"Hey there gorgeous." She jumped when a voice spoke to her.

She spun sideways and stared at Jamie in shock as

he slipped his cell phone into his pocket.

"What are you doing here?" she asked.

"I was just on my way to school." He pointed down the street. "Hey, are you okay?" he asked as he took a seat beside her on the bench. "You look freaked out."

That's because I am. She tried to calm her nerves, but he kept turning up when she was about to do bad things, and it was hard to keep her cool around him on a normal day. "What? No, I'm fine." She lied.

"You don't sound fine," he said, worry knotting his brow. "Can I help?"

"I doubt it." She gave in. She needed to tell someone about all of this. Maybe he could give her some good advice. "I have this test I have to pass, but I'm not sure it's the right thing to do." She admitted.

"Why do you think it's the wrong thing to do?" he asked.

"I don't. I guess I don't know enough about it, so I'm worried I'm doing something wrong." She was certain that if she knew why she was doing these things and what the result would be, she'd feel a lot better about it.

"But that's the point of tests though," he said. "You are never sure you got the answer right until you get the results. I think you're overthinking it. Just get it done and see what the results are." He smiled and held her hand.

She stared down at his hand. It was warm and bigger than hers was. He was right, of course. She didn't have all the answers yet, but she would when she completed her trials. "I guess you're right, thanks." She smiled back at him.

"Glad I could help. I need to get moving or I'll be late, but we're still on for tonight, right?" He released her hand and stood up.

"Eight o'clock." She nodded at him, feeling better about her trials as he blew her a kiss and continued down the street.

She watched him walk away until he was out of sight. Then she stood up with a sigh.

Trial two here I come.

7

LOST ILLUSIONS

ora stepped out of the elevator on the fourth floor and glanced around. The corridor was empty with only a couple of doors in it to choose from. She rushed past 4a and paused outside apartment 4b. There was no one around, so she knocked lightly on the door, listening for sounds of someone inside. The corridor remained silent.

She glanced down when the hard tile of corridor felt soft under her feet, noticing a welcome mat outside the door. It had a smiley face on it.

Oh, come on. How is this person bad?

With her heart pounding, she tried the door. As expected, it was locked. She pondered her options.

Breaking in wasn't going to be easy this time. She glanced down at the welcome mat again. *It can't be this easy,* she thought as she stepped off it, bent over and lifted the mat. Underneath was a shiny key. She shook her head.

Who does that anymore?

She picked up the key and weighed it in her palm as she considered what she was about to do. Bad enough breaking into someone's house, but cursing their clothes just seemed a step too far.

But Jamie said I should finish the test. Maybe this is to help the lady who lives here.

Dora inhaled deeply and let it out slowly before placing the key in the lock and turning it. The door unlocked easily. She pushed it open and stepped into the apartment, closing the door behind her. "Hello?" She called out to be certain she was alone.

No one answered. She walked through the apartment, feeling dirty on the inside. It was a cozy apartment with colorful walls and several throw cushions dotted around it. The decor made it seem far more welcoming than a cheap apartment should.

Just get the job done and get out.

She strode through the living area towards the doorway ahead that she suspected was a bedroom, trying not to think about what she was doing. Her eyes flicked over a small desk as she passed it, locking onto an open newspaper that resided there.

She froze and stared at the newspaper, recognizing the man in the photograph. It was Howard, the finance guy from her last trial. She frowned as she read the paper. He'd been arrested for embezzling millions from the company. He claimed he was innocent, and a hacker was responsible. It was an ongoing investigation.

Maybe he was a bad guy?

She picked up the newspaper and read more. Her eyes widened as she read the last line. He claimed a hacker had framed him with some kind of device.

What the hell?

The hard square feeling of the hex bag instantly jumped into her mind. She'd never looked inside the bag. What if it had contained a portable hacking device?

She decided that she needed more information before she did anything else. Something was very wrong with all of this. She pulled out the velvet bag of powder and opened it.

Fuck the consequences!

She touched the pale powder contained within, and her fingers tingled. Narrowing her eyes, she closed the bag. *Itching powder?*

What the hell kind of idiot uses that on someone's clothes?

She wondered as she brushed the powder off her hand and onto her combats.

She jumped when the phone rang, realizing that this was not the place to stop and think about her problems. After three rings, the answer machine picked up.

"Hi, this is a Cassie. Leave a message after the bleep." Her target's voice sang.

"Cassie, it's Jerry. I need to talk to you. I think Veronica is onto us. I told her I wanted a divorce, and she went ballistic. Just, be careful sweetheart. Once the divorce is over, we can move to Maui. I love you." A male voice said into the machine.

Veronica?

Dora wondered if it was the same Veronica she

had met last night.

It fucking has to be!

Anger settled over her. She hadn't been doing dark trials for a coven of witches. She'd been acting out petty revenge and committing crimes for a group of bitches!

She turned on her heel and stormed out of the apartment.

Time to pay those bitches a visit!

Dora stormed into the magic store and headed straight for the stockroom. She kicked open the door with so much force it slammed against the wall with a loud bang.

Loanda was hunched over her laptop. This time wearing jeans and a sweater, looking less like a witch and more like a soccer mom with her hair tied back in a tight ponytail. "What the fuck, Dora?" she cried, jumping out of her seat.

There was a scuffling noise in a room behind the storeroom. Dora shot a glance in that direction, wondering who was back there.

Veronica?

"I might ask you the same thing," she said, glancing back towards Loanda. "Embezzling money is your *magic*. That's your great power, a fucking hacking device?" She knocked over a few candles on her way towards the lying witch.

"I don't know what you mean," Loanda said, straightening her shoulders and relaxing her pose.

"Really? You don't? Well, the police will when I've finished telling them everything. Have a nice time in prison," Dora replied. "Oh, and like fuck I'll be doing any of your trials, you lying scumbag!" She turned to leave, shaking her head.

I can't believe I fell for this shit.

"You'll be arrested too. Your parents will love that," Loanda said.

Dora narrowed her eyes and spun around. "Leave my parents out of it. You don't even know them."

"The Reverend Theodore Carridine and his lovely wife Josie?" Loanda smirked. "I know them better than you think. What do you think they'll do to you when they find out you've been committing crimes for the devil?"

"Oh nice try. But I haven't, have I. I've been committing crimes for a skanky criminal with the demonic power of a cabbage, You don't fucking scare me. Tell my parents what you want. It won't stop me telling the police about you. Enjoy your time in jail, bitch!"

Loanda scowled before a spark of something dangerous lit her eyes. "Let me tell you what is going to happen. You're going to keep your mouth shut, and you're going to complete the final trial for me."

"Oh, yeah? Why exactly would I do that?" Dora tilted her head and scowled at Loanda.

"Because if you don't, my next sacrifice will be your boyfriend, Jamie." Loanda's eyes were glowing green.

Dora jumped as something heavy clattered on the floor in the back room. "How do you know about … I don't have a boyfriend. Have you been spying on me?"

"His life is forfeit if you don't do as I say," Loanda said in a deadly tone.

Dora was torn, but she didn't know how bad Loanda was.

Would she really hurt Jamie?

Loanda thrust a piece of parchment into her hand and grabbed her by the collar. "Do this last task, and you're free of all of this. Mess it up, and he dies," she hissed in her ear. Then she pushed her back, out of the room before slamming the door in her face.

Dora walked out of the magic store with panic bubbling at the back of her throat. She pulled her cell phone out of her pocket and dialed his number. It just rang and rang with no answer. *Shit!*

8

THOSE WHO BETRAY

Dora stared up at the full moon, clutching her trial in her hand. Loanda wanted her to retrieve the hacking device from Howard's office.

Of course she does because it will link her to it.

The serial number on it would give Howard's lawyers a paper trail to find the real culprit. By removing the evidence, she would be condemning Howard to a life in prison that Loanda deserved.

She sighed and shook her head. She liked being bad, but she couldn't do this. It would destroy Howard's life for no good reason. Her conscience would not allow it. On the flip side, there was Jamie. She couldn't find him. He wasn't answering his phone, and she didn't know how dangerous or desperate Loanda was. She had to assume that Loanda had already captured Jamie.

If I ever needed magic, now would be a good time for it to appear.

She stood in the dark street and shook her head.

Magic is bullshit. There's nothing in this world that I can believe in.

Disappointed by her own stupidity at believing in everything she'd been told, she scowled at the bag of powder in her hand.

It's all just an illusion.

She frowned for a moment. Maybe illusion was the answer. She shook the powder out of the bag and put her cell phone into it before tying the strings. She weighed the bag in her hands. It felt the same as the hacking device had. It looked the same as the hex bag.

It might work.

She nodded at the bag and slipped it into the back pocket of her combats. It was her only option. She walked down the street towards the magic store. Loanda had told her that Jamie was there, and she was holding him captive. If she gave Loanda the bag, she'd get Jamie.

Oh really? Then how will Loanda keep you quiet after that?

A shiver of fear shot up her spine. There really was only one way to silence someone, and she had no defense against that.

I'm sure I'll think of something.

With an impending feeling of doom, she pushed open the door to the magic store and stepped inside. For once, the room was brightly lit with harsh electric lighting. Loanda and Jamie stood in front of the sales desk. His hands were tied behind his back, and he looked scared.

"Uma! What are you—" He silenced when Loanda pressed a knife to his throat.

"Did you bring it?" Loanda asked.

Dora nodded and pulled the small sack out of her jeans pocket.

"Toss it over here," Loanda said.

"Give me Jamie first." Dora planned to grab him and make a run for it.

"At the same time," Loanda said.

Dora nodded.

Loanda pushed Jamie towards her, and he stumbled before dashing across the room to her as she tossed the bag to Loanda.

She didn't stop to see if Loanda caught the sack. She grabbed Jamie's arms and pulled him towards the door, intending to make a run for it, but he didn't move. "Come on!" she cried. He didn't budge.

She spun around to face him, and he flashed her a wide grin as he slipped his hands out of the ropes and waved them at her.

What the hell?

"What are you doing? She's going to kill us. Run!"

He grabbed her in his arms and spun her around to face Loanda, who hadn't moved an inch. She felt his hard chest pressing against her back, and his vice-like grip around her. His breath warmed her ear as he leaned over her. "Stupid girl," he whispered.

What's he doing?

She tried to make sense of what had just happened.

She felt him straighten up behind her. "What do

you want me to do with her, Ma?" he asked Loanda.

As she stared at Loanda's smiling face, she realized that more than magic was an illusion. Love was too.

Fuck!

Anger over his betrayal, and at herself for being so gullible, burned through her veins. She struggled and fought against his iron grip, kicking and biting to try to get free. His laugh in her ear just made her angrier and more violent. "Let me go, you son of a bitch!"

He growled and tightened his grip on her when she insulted his mother.

Good, I hope I hit a fucking nerve.

"Tie her up," Loanda said. "I need to find out if she told anyone about all of this."

Jamie dragged Dora over to an old wooden chair. He used duct tape to bind her wrists to the arms of the chair, and then knelt near her ankles. As he grabbed one ankle and taped it to the leg of the chair, she kicked him in the face with the other. He wailed in agony and fell backwards onto the floor.

She felt a blade press against her neck and saw Loanda's jeweled hand hover over her. "Don't move, or I'll kill you." Loanda's dulcet tones snarled into her ear.

Jamie got up off the floor and gripped her free ankle, binding it to the other leg of the chair. He scowled up at her, but she was pleased to see her footprint on his cheek. She tugged against the tape, but it wouldn't budge.

Okay, now I'm screwed.

It seemed hopeless. But even when she ran out of hope, she was too stubborn to admit defeat. "So, are you two dating then? Because I'd never expect a heifer to be your type," Dora said to Jamie.

He growled like an animal, and his mother scowled. "Don't speak about my mother like that, or I'll make you regret it." He snarled.

"Ohh, a momma's boy. That figures. You look the type," she said. She wanted to do some damage, and if all she had was words, then that's what she'd use.

"Screw you!" he cried.

"Not in this lifetime. Eww, I can't think of anything more pathetic than being near a whiny-apron-clinging-bitch-boy."

"Silence!" Loanda commended. "Don't listen to

her, Jamie. She's just trying to make you angry."

"Yep, listen to mommy. Just like you always do."

"You're going to die either way," Loanda said to her. "If you want it to hurt more, keep on talking." She flashed the knife and pointed at her eye. "It can be slow and painful, or quick and easy. Your choice."

Dora averted her eyes from the knife, the threat of dying silencing her for a moment. This was really happening. The thought of dying when she hadn't even lived yet was a sobering one.

She frowned as she noticed movement behind Jamie and Loanda. She quickly averted her eyes, so they didn't notice the other witches silently coming out of the back room. "So, is the whole coven in on this? I can only assume they are since you had me doing a trial for Veronica." She narrowed her eyes at Loanda.

"Those stupid women? They're not witches. They're bored housewives and idiots, especially Janet. No, I only sent you after Veronica's husband because she was becoming suspicious that the spells weren't working. Of course they weren't working! They were bullshit." Loanda laughed. "A bit of luck in Veronica's love life would keep her stupid. It doesn't matter now. We'll be gone soon, and they can pick up the mess I leave behind."

"Why does everyone call me stupid?" Janet said loudly.

Loanda and Jamie spun around to face five angry housewives, who had once thought they were witches.

"That's why," Veronica said to Janet, shaking her head. Then she fixed her cold eyes onto Loanda. "Your ass is about to get whooped, bitch."

Loanda backed away from the group with her hands held up. "Wait, you don't understand."

"You ready, ladies?" Veronica asked her coven, ignoring Loanda's pleas. They all nodded grimly and surrounded Loanda and Jamie.

Yes! Dora watched, feeling hopeful that she might survive this after all.

Janet lit several candles around the room before joining the group, who then proceeded to start chanting at Loanda and Jamie.

Shit! Dora sighed.

What the hell are they doing?

Loanda laughed as the group chanted around her.

"Dark and unholy mother, we pray to thee. Cast thy wrath upon our enemy. Unleash your vengeance upon these two, and take their souls to Hell with you." The witches repeatedly chanted the same lines.

Dora stared at the room as nothing happened.

Well, at least it rhymes, she thought, shaking her head.

Janet stumbled backwards as she had some kind of fit, knocking the candles over behind her. "I shall take all your souls." Her voice echoed out in a hollow tone that was much deeper than her usual one. The fallen candles must have landed on something flammable because the aisle exploded into flames, filling the room with smoke and heat.

Dora coughed, trying to get out of the chair. She couldn't see much other than flames and green-tinged smoke. She rocked the chair backwards to move herself away from the fire, but it tipped over and slammed back onto the floor, taking her with it. A wooden bound spell book landed on her chest, knocking the wind out of her as the bookcase behind her smashed through the window and into the street.

All around were screams from the people inside the building. Someone raced past her, narrowly missing stepping on her head to get out of the broken window behind her.

"Hold on there, son. Not so fast." She heard a male voice say, followed by the sound of a scuffle. She arched her head back to see an upside down view of the street. Chief Dawson and half of Berkville PD had appeared outside the store. They were cuffing Jamie's hands behind his back.

"Help!" she cried.

"Dora, what in the hell are you doing here?" Chief Dawson peered down at her.

"Long story." She shrugged.

Dad's going to kill me for this.

"Get everyone out, and call the fire department." The chief called out behind him as he grabbed her chair and lifted it out of the blazing store with her still tied to it. She felt the spell book fall from her chest and instinctively gripped it with her hand, taking it with her.

SPELL BOOK

D ora trudged into the church with her father and mother following her every move. She glanced back to try to explain. However, one look at her father's expression, and the words dried up in her mouth. His face was set in stone, and her mother refused to meet her eyes.

They marched her up to her room, following her into it without saying a word. When she turned around, she found both her parents standing in the doorway scowling at her. Their arms were folded, and their expressions were grim.

"Look, I know I messed up—" Dora began as she put the book she was holding onto her bed and sat down next to it.

"Witchcraft, crime and hacking!" Her father shouted.

"It wasn't real witchcraft, and I didn't know about the crime and hacking at the time." She tried to explain.

"Did you at least learn something from all of this?" Her mother narrowed her eyes.

"Belief is bullshit?" Dora guessed the answer.

Her mother and father both shook their heads.

"Nice boys suck?" She tried again.

Her father scowled, and her mother tutted at her.

Dora shrugged. "I got nothing."

"Oh you have something from all of this. You're grounded for a year, and you'll be having confession every Sunday from now on. You're not to call your friends or leave this room unless I say you can. There will be no internet, and no contact with anyone. You will go to school, come home and work. That is your life from now on. Do you understand me?" Her father bellowed.

She nodded and peered at her feet as her parents left the room, jumping slightly when her father slammed her bedroom door behind him. She'd got off pretty easy considering what she had done, even if it was unwittingly. Loanda had been arrested for embezzling from Howard's firm, and Howard had been released from custody. All charges against Dora had been dropped. The judge had classed her as an impressionable minor, who had mixed with the wrong people. Jamie had been given the ultimate punishment. He'd been sent to live with his father, Howard.

Veronica had divorced Jerry and bought the magic store with her divorce settlement. However, she'd banned Dora from the store and forced all the witches there to become Earth-loving naturists. Every dark and deadly element of the store had been destroyed. Now it stocked organic soap and recycled notebooks.

Dora, it seemed, was going to be punished by her parents for eternity, and she still hadn't found anything to believe in.

It was all for nothing.

She lay back on the bed and spread out her arms, feeling disappointed in everything. Her left hand brushed over the wooden bound book on the bed, tracing the strange symbols carved into it.

She sat up and stared at the book. It was encased in ancient wood, which was so old it had a green tint to it. The pages inside felt like cloth rather than paper. She flipped it open and peered inside. The book was filled with spells written in archaic English. Sketches of hellish faces and demons decorated each page. She frowned and read some of the spells in the book. She had never seen anything like it before.

She closed the book and stared at the cover. There were no words, just symbols engraved on it. The green cover glowed. She blinked, and the glow was gone, but she was certain she had seen it. She picked up the book and hugged it to her chest. It felt magical. Even though it went against everything she knew, she believed this book had magic in it.

What if this was what I was looking for all along?

Yeah, and witches are real. A sarcastic voice in the back of her mind said.

She sighed and dropped the book onto the bed. She wasn't going to fall for another illusion—she wasn't. She glanced down at the book. It had fallen open on a page titled: 'Speak to a Demon'. Her eyes flicked over the words on the page. It only involved lighting candles, shedding two drops of blood into a bowl and saying a short verse.

What the hell, right? It's not as if anything is going

to happen.

She grabbed a candle and a bowl of potpourri off her nightstand. She tipped the potpourri into the trashcan then placed both items on the carpet in front of her before sitting cross-legged in front of them with the grimoire beside her. She slid out her knife and pricked the end of her thumb, dropping two drops of blood into the bowl. Next, she pressed on her thumb to stop it bleeding.

Okay, let's try this.

"Demon of the darkest heart, I call upon your voice. If thy accepts my blood, then speak in tongues that I shall hear. Tell me secrets of old. Join with me and link our worlds. Show me the secrets of the dark." She read the spell aloud and waited. Her heart hammered, and the world seemed to blur around her for a moment. There was an eerie silence in the room, but she could hear voices screaming inside her head. Something washed over her, filling her body with power—something dark.

After a few moments, the voices faded, and the feeling evaporated. She held her breath as she stared at the bowl, waiting for something to happen. A few seconds later, she exhaled a sigh when nothing did.

Fuck!

"Dora, get down here and do the dishes, now!" She heard her dad calling up the stairs. She shook her head and stood up, turning towards the door. She stomped out of the room, leaving the book behind.

It felt like magic. I must have done something wrong.

She smiled as she left the room, feeling certain that the book contained magic.

I just have to learn how to use it.

"Dora, don't make me give you confession early!" Her father threatened.

And when I do, he's going to regret it.

As Dora left the room, the sigils of the book lit up and glowed green. Green smoke exuded from the pages and filled the room, swirling around and tainting the air.

THE END

READ THE PREVIEW FOR

AN AWARD-WINNING NOVEL IN THE DEMON DIARIES

Demonic
DORA

BEWITCHED IN HELL

CLAIRE CHILTON

1

HOLLOWED BE THY BRAIN

Dora Carridine rested her Doc Martens on the wooden church pew in front of her and idly cleaned her nails with a combat knife. She watched the small film crew set up around the podium at the front of the church while her father, the Reverend Theodore Carridine, had his hair fluffed into angelic white fuzz by a stylist.

She yawned. *Another bible bashing show coming soon to a TV near you!* She didn't ask for much in life, but she'd greatly appreciate it if the studio would cancel her father's embarrassing television show. She didn't pray to deities. Surely if there were such things as Gods, they'd have listened when she begged them to burn her mother alive for making her wear a cardigan in the eighth grade.

Dora had been a curious child, so when growing up in such a strict religious home, she'd tested out as many sins as she could. Lightning had never struck her down, she hadn't incurred the wrath of God and to be honest, if there was anyone up there watching, they didn't give a crap what she did.

"Now let us pray," her father said into the microphone when he stood at the podium, his face solemn.

Dora lowered her head and read the spell book in her lap. Images of demons and the blackest of magic filled the grimoire. She could barely read it. *I so wish I'd taken Latin now.*

"Our father, who art ..." Her father recited. The large congregation chanted with him.

"... Who art embarrassing whenst he is on television," Dora mumbled out of habit. Two devout parishioners spun around and glowered at her. "Hollowed be thy brain," she added for their benefit and chuckled when they turned away from her in disgust.

It was going to be a long show today, and she was already bored — beyond death. She glanced around the large church. People around her were praying with their eyes closed. Even her producer mother had her eyes shut and wasn't watching the show. *Time to get outta here.*

Dora shoved her spell book down the waistband of her red miniskirt and carefully lowered her feet off the pew. She slid the knife into the scabbard inside her boot before silently sinking down in her seat. She slipped onto the hard stone floor, rolling on all fours before she crawled through the narrow space between the pews. She sped up when she left the benches behind and was out in the open, scurrying towards the confessional boxes.

She rested behind the dark mahogany box before peering back at the room. No one was watching her. They were all standing and preparing to sing a hymn. She stood up and walked into the alcove ahead, then climbed the stone staircase towards her room.

She brushed the dust off the knees of her red and black striped tights on her way up. *Lazy ass cleaners should be crucified for the mess they left the place in.*

When she reached the top of the stairs, she turned left at the large organ pipes, heading up the narrow stone passage of a second staircase which led to her attic room.

Dora's room was pretty cool. It was inside the spire of the old church, offering her privacy from the rest of the world. She pushed open the ancient oak door. It made a loud, ominous creak – just how she liked it. The room was not decorated to her liking with baby pink walls and a matching carpet. The little princess room was her parents' doing. She couldn't count the number of times she'd spray painted blood-red pentagrams or black demon art on the walls of this room. Every time she came back from school, it was back to princess pink with decorative voile hanging over the bed and pink fluffy throw cushions on the furniture.

Bile rose in her throat when she glanced down at the pink floral-print duvet. She swallowed and knelt on the floor at the end of her bed before pulling out the large white plastic sheet from beneath it. The sheet was actually the back of a Twister mat, but it worked just as well for a dark arts summoning circle. She had painted a black and red pentagram on it to put it to a darker use than it was intended for, meaning she had to ensure it was well hidden from her parents at all times.

She shivered with excitement. Today was going to be her day. After years of trying and failing, she was finally going to cast a spell that would work. Despite years of failure, her inability to summon a demon hadn't dimmed her enthusiasm. The Wicca group at the local magical supply store would be laughing at her on the other side of their white-light Earth-mother faces if she pulled this off.

Dora was going to summon a demon, and not just a normal demon. No, she was going for a high-level demon that would be under her control. *The first thing he's going to do for me is make this room red.*

She placed six black candles around her makeshift summoning circle and lit them one by one. She put an ornate pottery bowl at the center of the circle and threw a mixture of herbs into it. Next, she pulled the knife out of her boot and made a small cut on her thumb with it. She watched her blood slowly drip into the bowl until there were six drops. Then she pressed her thumb against her leg. Once the cut had stopped bleeding, she dropped the knife and dragged her schoolbag over to her. She reached inside it, feeling for the small box in the bottom of the bag.

The secret ingredient was a Karabashi bloodstone. She carefully opened the small black box and stared at the red shiny stone in awe. It looked like a glass ball filled with blood. She'd searched high and low for one when she'd found the spell in her book. None of the usual haunts had one; not the antiques shop or even the specialist magic supply store. She had tried everywhere and had nearly given up altogether. One stormy night when she'd been staring at the dark skies, she'd had a moment of clarity. After some tough negotiation, she'd got it on Ebay.

Dora put the bloodstone in the bowl and picked up the grimoire. Her heart thundered in her chest. It was going to work, it was – she could feel it. She carefully read the spell and closed her eyes, chanting with a faith she'd never felt before. Six times she repeated the spell, and she waited.

She held her breath. A demon was going to appear — he was! Her clock ticked loudly as she sat cross-legged in front of her summoning circle, waiting. After a few silent moments, she let out her breath in an exhausted sigh. *Nothing again. Nothing ever works!*

She abruptly stood up and kicked over the bowl, shattering the bloodstone inside it. The thick, gloopy liquid slithered across the broken glass and mingled inside the bowl. She didn't bother to glance at it. She stormed out of her room and slammed the door shut behind her. *Nothing ever bloody works!*

Once Dora had left the room, a fire ignited in the center of the circle, and the Twister mat curled up as it became inflamed in the fires of hell.

HELL ON EARTH

osie Carridine watched from the front row pew as sweat dripped down her husband's face while he shouted at the TV cameras from the pulpit, threatening the wrath of God to all sinners. She nodded in agreement when he declared all vegetarians were an abomination. She was surely blessed to have such a righteous man for a husband. Not only had he saved her from a life of sin, pole dancing at the infamous 'Big Fat Joint', he'd also helped her career as a TV producer. Oh yes, life was wonderful once you left sin behind.

"And He shall strike you down," Theodore shouted out to his congregation. "Down to the depths of hell if – I-if …"

Theodore stopped speaking and stared at the back of the church with his mouth hanging open and his eyes widening. Josie jumped when she heard a loud scream from the back of the room. She spun around to look behind her while hearing the entire congregation shifting in their seats as they did the same.

Thick black swirls of smoke were twirling in the air around the closed doors of the church. *Has someone set the doors on fire?* She gaped at the fog in shock and shook her head at the thought. The mist wasn't behaving like smoke at all. It amassed into a big black blob with more and more seeping in under the door until it split into two foggy shadows.

She lifted her glasses, which were hanging around her neck, to peer through them. The two black smoky shapes formed into separate entities that appeared to have heads and arms. She dropped her glasses and rubbed her eyes before looking again.

At the same time, both shadows snapped open fiery red eyes. Their maws gaped as they let out a loud hollow laugh that echoed through the church.

Josie winced when Mrs Smiggins, the oldest member of the congregation, keeled over three aisles down. *I hope she's fainted, and she's not dead.*

The two shadows each gripped a handle of the double doors of the church and flung them open. A burst of flames shot through the entrance. Gale force winds blasted through the room, knocking parishioners over and sending the smaller ones flying around the church in a twister style hurricane.

Josie ducked down in her seat and hugged the pew, which was thankfully nailed down.

"Out, damned demon." She heard Theodore shout at the shadows, but they had already evaporated into the flames. Lightning shot around the high ceiling of the church, shattering through the stained-glass windows. The air was alive with electricity.

Josie fell to her knees and prayed – and this time she meant it. *Dear God, please save me from this nightmare. I promise to be faithful and end my affair with Phil on camera four. I'll remain good and pious, and stop trying to sell ad space on the church website. Amen.*

She glanced up to see an army of turquoise

serpents slithering through the doors and up the aisles towards the congregation, who were now screaming and running towards the pulpit to escape the demon snakes. She pulled herself up and jumped back as one of the snakes snapped at her hand, almost succeeding in ripping one of her fingers off. She pulled away just in time. They were like no snakes she'd ever seen before. Their eyes were ocean-blue, and their teeth were green. *Have they been drinking NiQuil?*

The snake reared up. It was as tall as she was. Fear slammed through her, making her knees tremble. It launched at her, emitting a deadly hiss. She threw her bible at it, knocking it backwards before she dashed towards the podium and cowered behind her husband, who continued to pray, although his voice was now hoarse.

The wind howled around them. The parishioners who hadn't passed out were all cowering around the pulpit. Some were white with shock, others were openly crying with thick trails of snot pouring out of their noses. They were the lucky ones, to have stuffed up noses. A few of the congregation had crapped their pants, judging by the stains on their clothes and the stench in the air.

Josie stared towards the blazing fires at the entrance as they wickedly licked the inside of the church. She glanced down the aisle in horror as her gaze fell upon the blue snakes writhing around at the foot of the raised pulpit, hissing and biting at each other. There was no way out.

She jumped when deep thunder echoed through the room and glanced up to see violent winds rip apart the inside of the chapel. Streaks of lighting shot around the small group of people huddled on the pulpit, making them scream and jerk in terror. Wailing pleas for God to help could be heard over the howling wind while the hurricane twisted its way up the church, about to engulf them.

Josie gasped at several loud stomps. The church shook violently before everything disappeared. The snakes vanished, the wind died down, the lightning stopped and the fire faded into nothing.

"Shit!" Dora cried as she walked back into her room and saw her carpet burning. She repeatedly stamped

on the fire until the last ember turned to black ash.

"Crap," she said. *Dad's going to go ballistic over this.*

Dora sighed at the useless summoning circle, which was now a curled up, burnt mess. She threw herself onto her bed and lay on her stomach, staring at the black screen of her pink television. She pulled the remote control from beneath the mattress and pressed the power button on it. Her TV was only allowed one network – her father's. She wasn't allowed to watch anything else. Thank Beelzebub her parents weren't net savvy, or she would be living in a religious bubble.

Since it was her bedtime, she knew the stupid show would be over soon. Sometimes the old black and white movies they showed late at night weren't too bad. Doris Day kicked ass in Calamity Jane.

The television flickered into life, and her dad's show appeared on the screen. People were wailing, crying, and praising the Lord. *Aww shit, they didn't do another one of those miracle cures shows, did they?*

Dora's eyes widened as Molly Carmichael, the

prim librarian from the main library, wandered in front of the camera mumbling incoherently. Molly turned her back to the camera and bowed to the pulpit. Dora's eyes widened more when she saw what she could only describe as effervescent shit stains decorating the back of Molly's pink tweed skirt. She watched Molly wander off camera, still mumbling random words like, 'snakes' and 'demons' as she disappeared from view.

For the first time ever, Dora found herself glued to her dad's show. *I can't believe I missed this.*

Her father finally came on screen as he pulled himself up off the floor. He clawed at the podium and dragged himself up, so his head appeared over it. He was shaking all over and had a few small cuts and gashes on his face. His hair looked like an oversized white afro hovering around his head. The priest's collar of his vestments hung limply down his neck in a white line.

"Dah …" He tried to speak, but his voice was so hoarse he only managed a sound. He was breathing hard. Judging by the murderous look in his eyes, Dora knew whatever he was about to say was not going to be good.

"Dohh ..." He managed before taking a deep breath. He stared down at the podium for a moment in silent fury.

He eventually looked straight up into the camera. The moans and wails of parishioners were echoing behind him, through the microphone. "D-Do-Dora, I'm going to kill you!" Her father gasped into the camera before he passed out on the podium and slid to the floor.

Dora blinked at the screen. *Shit, what am I getting blamed for now?*

3

INTO THE WARM AND STICKY

Kieron Lascher stopped chasing turquoise snakes when a burst of light exploded in the darkness a few feet away from him. He frowned and walked over to it. It was a hole ripped through the ether, a jagged tear of light in his dark and dismal world.

He reached out his hand and touched the shimmering light. It was warm and sticky. He pulled his hand back and glanced around him. There was no one around. Even the twittering hell spawn were up to no good elsewhere today. It wasn't surprising since it was only a couple of weeks until Judgment Day. Everyone was cramming for the finals.

Kieron knew he should be studying too. His father would eviscerate him if he failed this time. He had been revising all morning, trying to catch a snake for an experiment, but he had just ended up with several bites off the bloody things.

He tried not to let it bother him, but he was a failure at being evil. Nothing ever worked out. He got the formulas right, but it just never turned out evil enough. If he failed his test this year, he would be expelled from Hell. Everyone knew what that meant. A fate worse than colonic irrigation — he would be exiled to Earth.

Kieron had never been to Earth. He'd been born in Hell, but he'd seen it through the various portals. He shuddered at the thought of it. He'd seen the monotonous work humans had to do; filing, spread sheets … homework! Humans were sorry creatures; they followed dreams of things they'd never have, and they were powerless in the world they lived in. He couldn't imagine anything worse. No, he had to pass the test this year — being exiled to Earth was not an option.

He tilted his head while he studied the tear of

light. After a few minutes of contemplation, he decided the best plan was to fix it. It was dangerous leaving a gaping hole in the ether lying around like this. Someone might fall into it and hurt themselves.

He ran his fingers over the edges and encountered the warm sticky feeling again. *What kind of tear is it?* It pulsed as if it were alive. He'd never seen a portal like it, but there were a lot of lunatic demons practicing spells at this time of year. It was obviously a mistake because no talented warlock would create something so messy.

The wind howled around him in harsh, warm gusts. He glanced back and stared at the desolate horizon. *Are the volcanoes playing up again?* A vice-like grip clamped onto his wrist, which was still hovering over the tear in reality. He yelped when it tugged on his arm. The tear growled as it became a vortex, sucking things into it with howling winds and a terrifying force. Snakes and shrubbery shot past him as the growing hole consumed them. The ground shifted towards the portal, and the red sands of the barren landscape swirled around him. He attempted to scream but could only cough as the sand blew into his mouth.

He pulled back against the vacuum, trying to free himself from the portal, but the force was too powerful. He finally managed to cry out for help, but the sound was lost in the din. Using every muscle in his body, he tried to detach from the pulsing gash in reality. The power of the suction increased, lifting him off the ground before the portal pulled him into another realm.

Kieron squeezed his eyes shut as a blinding light flashed around him. His stomach leapt into his throat. The force of the pull flattened his cheeks to his skull. Every nerve in his body screamed in protest as gravity crushed it. He warily opened one eye, just in time to see the tear become a distant shadow. Flashes of bright lights sped past him. He crashed into something soft and expelled a shocked yelp of pain. Everything went dark as the portal closed.

He fought to suppress the urge to throw up while using his hands to search around in the dark. He could feel cloth draping over him and sharp painful blocks underneath him. He blindly explored his surroundings with his hands. The space was confined. He could feel the walls around him by simply stretching out his arms. He tried to control a bubble of panic when the thought of all those snakes being in here with him filled his mind.

His hand hit something on a string, a pendulum of some kind. He felt around for it in the darkness. It was wildly swinging around, but he caught it in his grasp on the third try. The heavy, metal object was hanging from twine. He tugged it to see if it would hold his weight. A bright light burst into the small room, and he found himself looking up the inside of a girl's dress. It would have been a pleasant experience had there been a girl inside the dress, but alas the dress was empty.

Something sharp dug into his backside, so he rooted around with his hands to pull the object out from beneath him. He stared at the shiny ruby slipper in his hand. The three-inch heel and pointed toe on the shoe answered some questions for him. *I'm in a witch's closet!*

Kieron pushed the clothes out of the way and got to his feet, ripping half of the dresses off their hangers in the process. He surveyed the inside of the closet before turning to face the slatted door. He inhaled a sharp breath when he stared through the gaps in the door and saw the witch.

She lay on a pink bed at the center of the room with her ebony hair twisted up in knots. Her blood-red lips pouted seductively at something she was watching. She was appealing to look at. Her long legs idly swung in the air behind her. She wore a pair of tiny red shorts and some kind of white tunic that had no sleeves. She was the first witch Kieron had ever seen, but his father had told him about them. They were all sexy little minxes with nasty tricks up their sleeves. He remembered seduction was their greatest trick, but he wasn't worried. He was pretty smooth with the ladies. He'd had the best tutors – succubae.

Kieron became aware of his own body swaying while he watched her legs swing back and forth behind her. *Hypnosis!* He realized and quickly averted his eyes up to the top of the closet, trying to calm his racing pulse. He refused to look at the witch and stared upwards. Piled on the shelf at the top of the closet were boxes and boxes of mysterious witch items. He tilted his head, trying to read the labels before reaching up to pull down the top box on the pile. It was red and white, the colors of blood and life. *It must be one of her darkest secrets.* It was labeled with one thick black word. He tried to pronounce the word in his mind. *Mono-Polly.* He didn't know this language, but it must be immensely powerful to have such colors on it. He took a deep breath and opened the box while his heart hammered.

Inside was an odd-looking ritual board. *What kind of casting can you do with this?* It had places on it with haunting names like 'Marylebone Station' and 'The Strand'. There were strange tarot cards called 'Chance' and 'Community Chest'. He recognized small silver ritual symbols of pagan items like the iron and the boot, but they were mixed in with symbols he hadn't seen before. He gasped when he picked up the small icon of a dog, dropping the box in shock. *What kind of monster is this witch? She'd cast upon a helpless hound.*

He nearly screamed when he looked through the slats in the door and saw her staring straight at him. She sat up on the bed and began making her way over to the closet. He inwardly cursed himself for making such a racket when he dropped the box.

He found his eyes drawn to her ample bosom when she stood up. *Think clean thoughts, think clean thoughts,* he told himself. *This minx will not turn me into her demon slave, no matter how bouncy they look. Er, she looks.*

He froze, overcome with a feeling of helplessness when she walked towards the door, reaching for the handle.

Her chamber door burst open, and a deranged holy man with wild white hair stormed into the room. He carried a crucifix in one hand and a bag of salt in the other. Kieron involuntarily hissed as the witch spun around to face the man, instinctively glancing down as his eyes were drawn to her ass.

"BACK DEMON!" Dora forgot about the noise in her closet as she spun around to face her father. He held a crucifix in front of him and appeared slightly crazed. His vestments were ripped and dirty, his hair was sticking out in a wild afro, and the insane gleam in his eyes could only mean one thing – exorcism time.

Dora backed away from him to the center of the room. "Dad, come on. Whatever I did, I didn't mean it," she said, holding her hands up in an attempt to placate him.

"SILENCE DEMON!" He bellowed before waving his cross at her.

"Oh, for fuc – ahhh …" Dora yawned in mid-argument. *Screw it, I can't be bothered. Just entertain his insanity, and you'll get to bed faster.*

She obediently stood in the center of the room while watching her father pour a circle of salt onto the floor around her. He shouted scripture at her, causing her to yawn again. Through bleary eyes, she studied him as he rushed to the wall and began nailing crosses to it around the doorframe. Sweat poured down his red face while he hammered the last cross into the wall.

He turned towards her, his knuckles turning white as he tightly gripped the bag of salt. "This will hold you, demon. Tomorrow you shall be sent back to Hell."

"Okay, Dad." Dora rubbed her eyes with her

fists, hoping he would bugger off soon, so she could go back to bed.

Her father lined the window ledge with salt, then the doorway before carefully stepping over it and leaving the room. "You'll burn for your sins." He told her before he closed the door.

"Okie dokie." She agreed as the door slammed shut. She shook her head at the insanity of her life.

Just before she stepped out of the circle, the door to her closet burst open. An attractive blond-haired boy with bright blue eyes fell through the door. He wore a swashbuckler's shirt and tight leather pants. "Don't worry, Minx-witch. I shall save you!" he cried.

Dora gasped and swung her fist out at the strange boy. Her fist made a solid connection with his jaw and sent him flipping over face first onto the floor. She looked down at his unconscious body and sighed. "Okay, if you must." She had a feeling it was was going to be a long night.

4

WITCHES & BITCHES

Dora studied the unconscious guy sprawled face down on her puce carpet. He was gorgeous even with his mouth hanging open and a bit of drool coming out of it. He had high cheekbones, a strong jawline, smooth tanned skin, broad shoulders and a perfect ass. She inclined her head sideways and checked out his backside. He was wearing a pair of tight brown leather pants. It was almost hypnotic watching his buttocks randomly flex.

She opened the leather pouch she had stolen from his belt. It was the closest thing he had to a wallet. It didn't contain money or any kind of identification, only a range of colorful gems. Given his choice of clothing and the contents of his pouch, she could only assume he was a crazy pirate. *That makes no sense. What would a pirate be doing in Berkville?*

The boy groaned, and she sighed with relief. She was glad she hadn't done any serious damage to him. He rolled over onto his back and gazed up at her with sleepy eyes. Little bursts of electricity tingled all over her body when his bright blue eyes scanned her from head to toe in lazy appreciation.

He smiled as he stretched his arms across the carpet, arching his back in the process. He paused when his fingers trailed over the circle of salt beside him. He briefly glanced at the salt and then back to Dora. His eyes widened in an instant, and his smile slipped. He jumped up yelping and frantically searching the room for something. "Oww! It burns, it burns," he cried, shaking his hand as if trying to get the grains of salt off it.

"What does?" She ran to his side to try and help, but he pushed her away during his desperate search of her room.

"Wash it off, the salt. Please, wash it off." He

begged as he wildly waved his hand around.

Dora snatched his hand out of the air, tightly gripping his wrist while she examined it. His palm was large and masculine compared to her small hands. The skin was smooth and tanned like the rest of him, but there wasn't a mark on it. It certainly wasn't burning. "It's not burning," she said as she showed him it.

He stopped dancing around like a lunatic and glanced down, peering at his hand in awe. Confusion furrowed his brow as she brushed the grains of salt off his palm.

"It's supposed to be burning." He peered up, and their eyes locked.

Her skin heated up, and a shiver trembled up her back. "Umm, why?" She attempted to appear unaffected by his close proximity.

"Because it's salt," he said, implying she should know what he meant.

Dora didn't know what to make of him. She just stared at him.

"Minx-witch, you should know these things." He told her.

"Who?" she asked. Why did he keep calling her that? His warm fingers massaged her hand before they traveled up to her wrist and arm.

"Okay, enough games," he said with defeat in his tone, but his eyes were sparkling with something else. "You win."

"Wha —" She didn't finish as he pulled her into his arms and kissed her. His hard body pressed against her, and his warm hands roamed up her back. She almost melted into his wicked kisses — almost.

Dora pushed him away. "What the hell do you think you're doing?"

"Becoming your willing slave." He winked at her and rested his hands on her hips.

Her heart did a little backflip. "Fine. Clean my room," she replied. *Heart, behave yourself. Who the hell is this guy?*

"Uh, I'm not that kind of slave. That's not my purpose."

"Your purpose? What the hell were you doing in my closet? Who are you?" She stepped back and untangled herself from his embrace in case he attacked her again. She could handle many things;

violence, robbery even religious zealots, but someone being nice to her and kissing her was a whole new experience.

"Oh, how rude of me." He dipped his head in a short bow before raising her hand to his lips and kissing it. "Let me introduce myself. I am Lord Kieron D. Lascher."

Dora snatched her hand back before he kissed anything else and caused her brain to shrink. "What does the 'D' stand for?"

"Oh, er, Derek," he mumbled. "And you are?"

"Derek?" She expelled a surprised giggle.

"It means ruler." He appeared offended. "What's your name, Minx-witch?" he snapped.

"Dora Carridine."

"Hmm, and *you* mock my name?" Kieron pouted at her.

"Sorry," she mumbled, laughing. "It was fun – wait. Who the hell are you and what were you doing in my closet? Did Dad put you in there?"

"Does your father often put young men in your closet late at night?" Kieron asked. He appeared genuinely curious.

"Er, not so far, but you never know with him."

"I cannot confirm who put me in your closet, for I do not know. But I was ripped from my home and brought here for a reason. The longer I am here, the more I realize that it was the fates that sent me." He studied her for a moment. "I believe I have been sent here for you. In fact, I am sure of it."

The words made something inside Dora heat up, and a shiver trembled through her body. Maybe it was because he looked so honorable and hot when he said it. Also, what girl wouldn't love a guy that fate sent to her?

"What makes you think that?" she asked.

"You clearly need saving. It is simply a question of from what?" He slowly walked around her. "You are a minx-witch who is trapped in a tower by an evil holy man. Perhaps I am to save you from him?"

He'd been standing behind her for a while. She wondered what he was doing back there, so she spun around and caught him staring at the place her ass had been a few moments earlier. She scowled at him.

"Clearly you are also lacking in your skills as a minx if your kisses are anything to go by. Perhaps my duty is to teach you seduction." He grinned as he leapt at her, knocking her onto the bed and pinning her down by the wrists. "Would you like that?"

Dora acted on instinct. She kneed him in the balls as hard as she could before pushing him off her.

He rolled sideways onto the bed and curled up in agony. "Why would you do that?" he cried. "What kind of demon-witch are you?"

"One who is perfectly capable of taking care of herself," she replied as she got off the bed and picked up a heavy vase. "Try that again, and I'll knock you senseless – again!"

He held up his hands in submission and sat up on the bed. "So, why am I here? Why else would I be here if not to help you?" He appeared to be genuinely confused.

"Where did you come from?" she asked. She needed to know who this guy was. All she knew so far was he used old-fashioned words, and he was a bit of a perv.

"Hell," he said, waving his hand in the air as if to brush the question away. "Sinner's Hall, the fifth level."

Dora stared at him in awe. "Hell? Y-y-you're a

demon?"

"Obviously," he said, appearing a bit upset that she hadn't already known that. "Can't you tell by my evil ways?"

"Well, er, no." She studied his handsome face and attractive body. "Aren't demons supposed to have horns?"

"Only hell spawn have them on the outside. The main demons are just –"

"Horny?" She cut in.

Kieron flashed a wicked grin.

Dora shook her head. "I can't believe I ask for a demon lord, and I get *you*."

"Hey! I am a demon lord." He shot her an annoyed glance. "A big evil one, a master of destruction …"

She peered in her closet. "Dress destruction?"

"That wasn't my fault."

"Uh huh, how exactly are *you* evil? You came here to save me!"

"And to defile you, of course." He defended his evil ways.

"Okay, so … I summoned you. That makes you my bitch, right?"

"I do not know that term." He sounded confused.

"Bitch? It means slave or servant, but in a good and manly way." Dora grinned.

"Ah, I see. Yes Minx-witch-Dora, I am your bitch."

She stifled a giggle. "Right then, *My Bitch*, there will be no defiling of me, and you will do as I command, understand?"

"Not even a little bit of defiling?" A disappointed expression appeared on his face.

"No, none at all."

"Evildoing?" His blue eyes shone with hope.

"There probably will be some evildoing." She admitted.

"Okay, that sounds good." Kieron agreed.

"Good. Now, I'm tired. It's been a really long day, so I'm going to go to bed, and I suggest you do the same." She told him before she climbed into bed and hugged her pillow.

The bed trembled as he got off it, and she snuggled under her blanket. The bed bounced as a weight landed on it. A hot body pressed against her back, and a strong masculine arm snaked around her waist.

"Bitch."

"Yes, my minx." His hot breath warmed the back of her neck.

"What are you doing?"

"Sleeping."

"Not in my bed."

"Oh come on! What's a shared bed between a master and their minion?"

Dora rolled over and pushed him off the bed with as much force as she could muster.

"Fine." He snapped, pushing himself off the floor. "I'll sleep in the closet."

"Good bitch," she said, stifling a laugh as he stomped over to the closet, walked into it and slammed the door shut behind him.

After a few minutes, she began to worry about Kieron. *There isn't enough room in the closet for him to lie down.* With a sigh, she climbed out of bed and walked over to the closet door, deciding he'd be fine with a sleeping bag on the floor, instead.

Dora opened the door while trying to think of the best way to suggest he should sleep on her floor. She blinked at the scene inside her closet. Kieron lay on a round king-sized waterbed adorned with red silk sheets and an array of opulent pillows and blankets. The closet had been transformed into a large room with everything from a minibar to a couch fitting comfortably inside it.

He glanced up at her with a devilish grin. "I knew you'd change your mind, my frisky little minx. There's room for two." He winked.

"Bitch," she said before slamming the door on him. She walked away from the closet and climbed back into her pink bed, hugging her blanket and trying not to think about devilish demons.

Sleep, she told herself. *Maybe when I wake up the world will be sane again.*

READ MORE

Buy the book online at:

WWW.CLAIRE-CHILTON.COM

After being expelled from Hell, she woke up in her own coffin...

When Dora Carridine wakes up in her coffin, the first thing she plans to do is find out what happened to her friends since they were also exiled from Hell. But Dora didn't come back entirely human, and everyone keeps trying to kill her.

If she manages to avoid being bitten by an over-amorous, Victorian vampire, being captured by the Vatican and being roasted alive by her neighbors, then hopefully she can find Kieron and find out what she really is.

But first, she has to put an end to an ancient war amongst the paranormal beings on Earth. How hard can that be, right?

OUT NOW

WWW.CLAIRE-CHILTON.COM

CONTINUE READING WITH

A BESTSELLING NOVEL IN THE DEMON DIARIES

Divine DORA

BEWITCHED IN HEAVEN

CLAIRE CHILTON

Heaven just turned out to be worse than Hell!

After being killed, Dora Carridine was shipped off to Heaven, but she's not ready to give up her life just yet, especially not when it means spending eternity in Angel boot camp.

She does everything in her power to try to get home, but nothing works. Even if she manages to escape Camp Angel and survive the sadistic drill sergeant, she still doesn't know how to get her body back.

Powerless and alone, she decides that there is only one thing she can do. Dora has to find God, and hope he's not a sanctimonious dick.

WWW.CLAIRE−CHILTON.COM

CAN'T WAIT FOR CLAIRE CHILTON'S NEXT STORY?

Let her know by leaving stars and telling her what you liked about

A HINT OF MAGIC

in a review!

FREE BOOKS

Enjoy Claire Chilton's free books. Try out her other series for free or read more of this series on any device with **Free Reads**.

claire-chilton.com/free-books

WANT TO TALK TO OTHER FANS?

Visit *claire-chilton.com* and join the discussion.

AUTHOR

After completing her honors degree in English Literature, Claire Chilton was interviewed to work for MI5. Fortunately, for the sake of the United Kingdom, she did not get the job. Now a web designer and graphic designer with a passion for great stories, she writes about the adventures she'd like to have.

A prolific writer with wide-ranging interests, Claire specializes in romantic and speculative fiction, which includes genres such as mystery, science fiction, fantasy, horror, comedy and romance. Her mystery romance novel, *Hustle*, won Harlequin's *So You Think You Can Write* contest in 2013, and her previous books in *The Demon Diaries* won the *Most Read* award on Wattpad.

After exploring the world in her misspent youth, traveling across Europe, Africa, and the Caribbean, she now lives in an ancient Roman city in Yorkshire with her Californian husband and a fluffy kitten called Shadow, who is convinced she is a bigger cat than she is.

You can find Claire online at **claire-chilton.com**.

www.ingramcontent.com/pod-product-compliance
Lightning Source LLC
Chambersburg PA
CBHW020404130626
46549CB00006B/2433